Carolyn's Circus

FROM THE DEEPEST DARKEST
CONGO, COMES A GIFT

CLANCY JOHN IMISLUND
AND FREESE, J.S.P

Acknowledgement

John and I would like to deeply thank all of those that have helped us along the way. These people include **Diane, Mary, Mary** (Yes. Two of them!), **Charlotte, Christine, Annie, Sally, Theresa, Paul, Shane,** and a host of others who nitpicked every typographical error, punctuation snafu, plot paradox, or otherwise misleading direction our destruction course of the English language decided to lead us. Without their chewing gum in all the breaches of our rickety sloop, we would not have made it past the breakwater in a drainage gutter. Though we all missed a few (GRRRR!!!), It floated long enough to get us all here.

The Tea Parties of Shraugh

In the country of Ireland, there is a small town near the area of Shraugh in the county of Clare. This town is surrounded by meadows and farm lands as far as one dares travel. This is a quiet place with pub, market, and farming supplies all at arm's reach --The people here well acquainted and sharing. They participated in all aspects of life together. There are many families here but there happens to be an extra special one for they are meant to unearth an ancient secret. There is nothing else unusual about them except for their future.

In this town lived a family by the name of Catlin. They seem like a regular family on the outside but the Irish are very good at keeping up appearances. A surprise was always around the corner with them though.

The father's name was John. He was a very hard working man and traveled the world on his quests for various artifacts and unique items. He had gone as far as China on his adventures and returned with many interesting pieces of antiquity. His best finds adorned the mantle of the fireplace in their home including a rare alabaster vase and a Terracotta warrior from some small city near the Great Wall—his pipe he was honored to place next to them. These objects really have nothing to do with upcoming events in this story but they are there to show the lengths that John would go to keep his family housed and fed. He was a good and loving father though sometimes his quests kept him from his family for longer periods of time than expected. Luckily, he had a very strong and brave woman to manage the household when he was away. This woman, his wife, was given the name, Maeve.

Maeve was the name of a mythical Irish queen. This queen was able to outwit and defeat one of Ireland's finest and strongest heroes—Cuchulain. Maeve's parents noticed this strength in her on the day she was born and took no time to conjure the name.

John's wife lived up to the billing. She was a very austere and thorough educator at the house where she taught. All of the faculty and children knew not to cross Maeve. "Do you want to end like Cuchulain?" they would whisper. Even the people at the market were careful not to short-change Maeve even a half-penny. They learned not to try to give her extra portions in some effort to crack her strict shell either. "I will take what I pay for and not morsel more or less." she would say in a very commanding and proud tone. Even the milkman knew to fill the bottles to just the correct level and to place them to an exact spot on the porch of the cottage where Maeve and her husband lived. The milk had to be there at a specific time in the morning or Maeve would not take it or pay. People thought her cruel and without feeling and wondered what John ever saw in her. They believed he had married a witch that cast some class of evil spell on him. This surely must be.

What the people of the town did not know is that Maeve had a gaping hole in her armor that only her husband could see. There was another element of the family that exposed this weakness. This element came in the form of their only child and beautiful daughter. The name given to this child was Carolyn.

Carolyn was a vivacious and happy child. She could always create fun from nothing though this got her into some trouble at the school. Her marks were less than the best it was easy to notice. Her bedroom was always disheveled and Carolyn was often lazy about performing her chores. Carolyn loved to hold tea parties almost every day in the meadow behind the cottage where they lived. She had a select group of close friends that were always in attendance—laughter and play throughout. There was always another attendee at these parties. This was Carolyn's mother.

Maeve was more enjoined with her daughter's hijinks than any of Carolyn's friends. Carolyn could do no wrong in her mother's eyes and they often kept playing and laughing long after Carolyn's friends had returned to their homes. They invented and played many games late into the night especially when John was not there to get Carolyn into bed at a reasonable time. They laughed and played until they fell asleep in the family living room. Carolyn did have to get to school in the morning though and Maeve made sure Carolyn was always fed a warm breakfast and was properly dressed for the elements. Maeve did not walk with Carolyn to school—she allowed Carolyn's friends to do this.

Carolyn attended the school where her mother taught and was in classrooms with her every day since she was old enough to participate. The other children felt sorry for Carolyn. How unfair was this for a child to be forced to be made to sit in these conditions? Maeve was the strictest teacher of the whole school and she was especially hard on Carolyn—Nothing Carolyn did was good enough for Maeve in the classroom. Carolyn was often late coming back from breaks and this earned Maeve's ire even more. The other children shied away during Maeve's outbursts towards Carolyn. It was very painful to witness. How could Carolyn keep a smile on her face after that? Even Maeve's colleagues were upset and worried. What a terrible time this child must be having. It was profanely sad – or so they thought.

This was a game that Carolyn and her mother had concocted during one of their frequent play sessions. It was very clever and an act. Maeve and Carolyn knew the routine and were very good at it by now. They often laughed late into the night while discussing Carolyn's transgressions in the classroom and Maeve's fierce reactions. It was an art form that Maeve knew would keep Carolyn from being bullied at school -- No "teachers pet". Carolyn and her mother were so closely bonded and in-sync now that even John scratched his head in confusion to see them together and hear them laugh. It was almost like they were a single person in separate bodies. The Irish are very mystically inclined so John was well acquainted with such things. This went far beyond that and to say "Soul Mates" is a disservice. To baffle the Irishman such as John with such things is quite a feat. John was wise and thought "If it works then I best be keepin' my long snout out of it.". This he did.

So it was a golden time in the Catlin household for many years. John marvelled at how Carolyn had blossomed. He cared not about her grades or the mess in her bedroom. His wife and daughter were as happy as could be and it made him a bit jealous not to be part of it. It did make him feel a little more comfortable knowing his family was so arranged.

Soon, he would have to take another long and dreary voyage to haggle for more rarities. He had nothing to worry about.

There did come the day when some unusual news arrived. John was returning from a business trip to a land Maeve could not even pronounce. Once again, Maeve tended to the post. An odd letter arrived in the midst of a tea party in the meadow. The postman seemed quite adamant that Maeve take a specific parcel. It must've been something very important as the postman never did things such as this. Carolyn was baffled and surprised to see her mother's reaction to the news. It was few and far between that she ever saw her mother with a frown like the one that came from the parcel. Maeve politely excused herself from the party and went into the cottage. Carolyn was terribly curious now but the tea party went on as planned. Carolyn's friends still laughed and played but they did notice that she was not engaging. She seemed concerned and pensive.

There was no laughter or games that night and that intrigued Carolyn further. John came home that evening and was surprised to see them not engaging in the usual shenanigans. Carolyn and Maeve already asleep by 9 pm? This was definitely odd.

In the morning, Carolyn came down to breakfast as ever. Her mother and father were embraced – each with a scowl and a look of consternation. The parcel from the day before on the table in front of John. Carolyn smiled and tried to and understand but she was terribly confused. What could be in that note? Her mother left the room very quickly and went to her bedroom. Her father held a sad look as he watched his wife leave the dining table. He then turned his gaze towards Carolyn and tried to smile. This was not fooling her at all. She became far more confused as her father fumbled for words. He was finally able to get out "Dear, please get to your room. I will be up to check in on you later.". Carolyn tried to smile back and say "Yes, daddy." but this was just a facade. As soon as she turned her back to go, the fake smile turned almost into a poker stare. "Why is Ma not nestling me in tonight? I have never seen her cry either. I will ask daddy tonight when he comes around. Daddy will tell me.". John never came to Carolyn's room that night and she finally drifted off into a very calm and deep sleep—her dreams not so pleasant, however.

In the morning, Carolyn awoke on her own. Neither her mother or father were present—this was rarer than a four-leafer in a plague of locusts. Carolyn slowly got dressed—Very methodical and serious about it as well. She would certainly go downstairs this morning and discover the reasons for the previous evening's spectacle. She was resolute. She could smell the breakfast so she knew her parents were there. She would fix this now.

As she approached the table, her father was there and sipping a cup of tea. Carolyn could smell that this was his "special" tea that he would drink when problems seemed to be overwhelming for his family. Her breakfast was ready and warm so she sat down and said "Good morning, daddy!". Her father just mumbled "Mornin'..." and continued to stare at his tea. Carolyn had seen her father like this before so she knew this was not the right time to start asking questions. She would try anyway. She also noticed a packed suitcase and umbrella placed by the front door. She asked with a smile "daddy, are you going out on one of your trips again?. After a short moment, he merely half-whispered "Ah…no… Your mother has to leave us now for a while…". He continued to stare at his tea. By the sound of it, the tea was already taking effect. Carolyn decided to ask him no more questions. She noticed the opened parcel on the mantle so she would read it when her father went to take his nap. The tea always made him do this. She was not finished with this yet.

Carolyn went back upstairs to give her father some time. She would polish her shoes and play with the new dolls her father had brought to her from a faraway land whose name she could not pronounce. These would be the guests of honor at today's tea party. Everything would be perfect again this afternoon as it was a beautiful Saturday in Shraugh. Her mother sparkled on such days. Carolyn drifted away to sleep and dreamed of the party. Oh how these fancy toys would please her friends and mother. This would be the best party yet!

When she awoke, she felt rushed but rested. It was time for the party to commence and the other children would be arriving within the hour. Hopefully her mother had taken care of the preparations. Carolyn put on a fine dress and ran downstairs to start things moving. Unusually, there was no smell of tea brewing and no crisps on platters waiting. Her father's door was closed so his nap continued. She also noticed that the bag and umbrella were gone (Mother must have put them up) but the parcel was still on the mantle. This was a good time to read it so Carolyn went to fetch it. She carefully opened it—cautious to peek down the hallway and make sure her parents did not catch her reading something not addressed to her.

She tried her best but she could not understand a word of it. There were many big-people words that made no sense to her and some of them were blurred from her mother's tears. This was ultimately frustrating and Carolyn was beginning to feel things she had never felt before. She heard a shuffling in the hallway so she replaced the parcel and sat in a reading chair. Her parents will explain it to her now. Her face was not smiling anymore. The commotion was just her father come to refill his tea and return to his room.

No children came over that day and there was no tea party...

From the Darkest Congo, Comes a Gift.

A few days of this, then weeks, and Carolyn would always sit in that chair when her father was around. She waited patiently until he was ready to speak of it. It was her mother's chair and her father had to pass by it whenever he came and left the house. He was always nice to her and said sweet things to her when he passed by. Carolyn acknowledged this but she was not there for that. She could be eternally patient—a trait she learned from her mother. John was fully aware of what Carolyn was doing and what she wanted. This was not the only change in her behaviors that he noticed.

He also noticed that Carolyn never called him "daddy" anymore. She would address him as "father"— A very prim girl now. Carolyn was always perfectly clean—No more skinned knees and muddy clothes from playing with her friends in the meadow. Her room was absolutely ordered and spotless now. Carolyn spent hours on this. She always finished her meals, washed her dishes, took her bath, and put herself to bed as a clockwork. Her schooling had also improved. Carolyn now always had the highest marks. She was even made to bring home notes of commendation and accolades. One funny note came home with her one day written by the replacement teacher at Carolyn's school. It read:

"Dear Mr. Catlin,

When I took this assignment, I was told to watch out for a rambunctious child by the name of Carolyn. I was coached and picked because I know how to deal with such children. I must say though that a joke has been played on us both. She is the most dedicated and studious of the class. She is never late and never makes a peep unless she is answering yet another question. These questions baffle her classmates but not Carolyn. I must say she is the finest student I have ever encountered in my 16 years at this profession. I must wholeheartedly congratulate you on the job you are doing at home. Your family is an example for all of the people of Shraugh. I thought you should know.

Best and thank you,
Sr. Shannon Leigh"

For most parents, this would be exciting and happy news. It was scarce for instructors of this particular institution to be sending such notes— and it was a woman of the cloth doing the sending. Carolyn was bringing them home at least twice a week and this was yet another special day. Not the case for John. He knew his daughter very well and loved her but this was so unlike her. Carolyn had also developed a new routine that John thought quite odd. She would go out at the same time each day and wait at the bus stop just down the road. She could sit there for hours. John knew that she was waiting for her mother to return though he never asked her why she perched there. He would often go out and sit with her. He attempted to make stabs at conversation but Carolyn was very curt (not rude though) and with only a paucity of words. John learned to be patient and silent around her during these vigils. It was at these times that John could reason things out. She was completely self-controlled now. She kept her room and herself clean. She was extremely punctual. She was never angry or sad. She was earning top marks for her demeanor and schoolwork. What else could a parent ask for? He should be overjoyed. John knew he was trying to fool himself and that it was failing. He needed a break.

A break did come in a roundabout way. One afternoon, another parcel came for John. Carolyn was sitting in the reading chair again staring at him intently. After reading the note, he turned to Carolyn and relayed its contents to her. The staff at the museum needed John's services at a new excavation site and he was asked to report within the week. This was in an Arab land that John had visited many times and most of the traders there were like his second family. They only haggled for fun. Carolyn just stared.

John knew that there were people he could rely on to watch after Carolyn in his absence. Maeve had two sisters— one older, one younger. They were called Charlotte and Mary and they adored Carolyn. They were sometimes even better playmates than Maeve. He would contact them this evening. Carolyn, though usually excited about such news, was nonplussed. It would be okay he assured her. It was time for their trip to the bus stop and vigil so he walked with Carolyn and participated as ever. Later, they would have dinner and Carolyn would graduate to her room. John would take that time to contact her aunts and pack his bags. He would leave in the morning as he wanted to expedite the execution of this latest journey to be back.

When the morning came, the aunts arrived and Carolyn greeted them cordially and politely. "We are gonna have such fun together my dear!" they cackled. Pixies and wood spirits them both to rival Maeve. John was satisfied so he went to his room to gather his things. The bus to Shannon would be arriving in 20 minutes so he kissed Carolyn and her aunts goodbye and told them he would write to them every day. He began the walk down to the bus stop but then an odd thing happened.

When he turned to see Carolyn running from their cottage towards him, he slowed down so as to allow her to catch up. She stopped and stared for a few seconds but then uttered the words "Please bring home to me something very special". She then hugged him and said "I love you, father." before quickly running back to the cottage. John wanted to shout back but he was too stunned. He could see the bus coming over the faraway hill so it was time for him to leave. He sure had much more to ponder now. These thoughts would make the trip pass quickly or so he hoped.

The voyage took him through lands that he had visited many times before—England, France, Turkey, Syria, Israel, and eventually down to the southern regions and the Arab trading hub. He had done much business in each of these places and had many adventures. He always made sure that he had a letter to Shraugh in the post describing his past activities pertinent to these regions. He did this religiously as he had promised Carolyn and her aunts.

After a day and night of long rest, John made an appearance to the new excavation site. He saw many of his friends there and they haggled as ever over a new collection freshly discovered. Most of these were baubles already in his lockers back home. He knew he could sell these in Paris and London. One item caught his attention, however. It was a bronze effigy of the Hindu god Ganesh. John knew this was a rare find in these parts as it came from the far-east. He kept it downplayed and seemed disinterested. This tactic fooled his fellow traders and won him the haggling and the statue.

Ganesh was known to be the god that could triumph over any obstacle with huge leaps and bounds—defiant and invincible. This might be just the thing he needed to assuage Carolyn back in Shraugh. This one he would not sell at Piccadilly-"Very special" indeed.

When the evening came, John made the rounds through the local villages to meet with old friends and swap stories over rare potions. He bragged of his statue and his talents as a rooster crows. This caused much laughter. Carolyn was still on his mind, however.

John only had one last visit to make that evening. This one was always the last when he was in such a part of the world. It was the tent of the tribal leaders and top traders. Although this was a difficult meeting for others to arrange, John never had a problem getting a seat at their table. They loved his wit, charm, and potion-fueled long-winded tales—always embellished. It was here that John told Carolyn's story and of her difficulties. The leaders were politely silent and listened. They were also flashing knowing glances at each other as John continued his tale of woe. At the conclusion of this saga, the room was deadly silent. They passed around a pipe as John stared vacantly at the stars. One man left the table and exited behind a curtain. In the quiet room, John could hear voices. It must certainly be about the Ganesh he'd woven in.

John was sleepy now and it was time to retire. He would prepare his things for his voyage back to Ireland in the morning. His mission was a success.

...or so he thought. The man that had left the table earlier emerged from behind the curtain and quickly waved for John to come over. This was unusual because John knew who was behind that curtain. He walked furtively in that direction and the entire room was now staring at him now. It was rare to get an audience with the tribal chieftain so John immediately took the opportunity and went into his chambers. There, he disappeared for an unknown amount of time. When John finally did return from behind the curtain, he left the trader's tent without a goodbye. He had a blank look on his face as he walked towards his own tent. What the chief had told him was mysterious and a little frightening. He would receive his morning instructions through dreams tonight. The Irish are spiritual and superstitious but this was a little too much, even for John.

In his dreams, the first spoke of a magician. This magician could be found by heading west to small a village south of the city of Cairo in Egypt. More strange is that the further dreams told him that his camel would know the way. "But I don't have a camel!"—dreams have no logic though. John also dreamed of stars and moon in configurations that would lead him still further towards another destination. These dreams were extremely vivid and lucid. John did notice that this was the first night he had not dreamed of Carolyn.

John awoke in the morning to a growling, bellowing sound. He slowly got up and went to go look for the source. Outside of his tent flap, a large white camel stood staring at him. It brayed again when it recognized John and shook its head. John suspended belief and wasted no time packing up his tent and gear and getting the camel ready for wherever this was going to take them. John carefully mounted the camel as he was a horseman in Ireland and camels were somewhat odd beasts to him. The camel uttered a third bellow and bray then slowly started moving westward. John believed this a long journey ahead so he just sat back and let the stuff of his dreams play out. It would also give him time to write another letter or two to his family in Shraugh.

John lost all sense of time as he went briefly into long periods of naps and dreams. These were all about Carolyn and not as real as those from the night before. Night was falling now and John thought this would be a good place to spend the night. He pulled on the reigns with a "whoa!". The camel brayed again and plodded on still. A horse would definitely need a rest by now. Camels are odd beasts indeed. John's watch had stopped a while back but he figured the camel would get tired soon. It must've been a long time. John had slept during the day but strangely enough, he drifted away again. The camel plodded on…

John was awoken again by the braying and bellowing gift-camel. It was still night. Was it the same night? What day is this? Where am I? The camel had stopped and kneeled. John noticed a small hut in an otherwise uninhabited place. This must be the place the dream spoke of. John dismounted the camel and approached the hut. There was a light on inside so he stopped just before another loud, prodding bray from the camel drove him further. John entered the hut expecting to see a magician if the dreams were correct. They had been so far.

Sitting by a fire was a small woman but otherwise nothing unusual. The woman smiled and waved him over to sit with her. John accepted with a nod as he did not know the language this woman might speak. She offered him a cup and John accepted—A cool drink and it was very relaxing and refreshing. After a swig or two, John decided it was time to speak with this woman. He felt the old stories welling up in in him and he was ready to regale whether the woman understood him or not. John knew he was good at using his body to tell stories too. Most of the traders he spoke with on his adventures did not understand one of his flowery words but John's hand-waving and facial expressions always brought a smile from Kerry to Peking.

Before John could get his first word out, the woman placed her hand over his mouth and smiled. She said, in the clearest English he had ever heard, "I know why you are here, Irishman. I have something for you.". She removed her hand, refilled his cup, and bade him drink again. This John did. She waited a moment with a smile on her face and then arose. She went to a strange looking box that seemed to appear from nowhere. John hadn't noticed it on his way in but that was probably because of his exhaustion. The woman returned from the box and showed John a necklace with an amulet affixed. He was curious and attempted to speak again. She put her hand over his mouth for the second time -- still holding her smile. She placed the necklace around his neck and said to John "This is what you need.". John noticed that the necklace heavy – heavier than usual for something that size. He went to speak a third time but the result was the same. With her hand over his mouth, she told him one last thing: "The amulet is heavy because your heart is heavy. When it takes you to where you need to be, you will see a beautiful change. Remember the stars and the moon from your dreams. You will seek a green fire". John thought about this but never again about speaking to the magician. His head was heavy now too so he leaned back and fell asleep. There were no dreams this night. Green fire?

John awoke again at sunrise. As he had many times, he was in his comfortable and reliable tent – his items carefully arrayed around him. He wanted to sleep a little while longer but then he jumped up with a start. Where was he? Where is the hut? He remembered it all so perfectly. He ran out of the tent to look around. There was no hut and the camel was gone. There were no footprints anywhere. This long jour-ney and the magic potions were affecting his mind as these dreams were becoming more real. Oh, to be back in front of his hearth with Carolyn again. He would sleep for a month on his return.

He surveyed the area around him. There was nothing but large dunes and sand as far as one could see. It was time for him to go home now. He had overdone it on this excursion and he began packing up his things for the long voyage home.

A pair of objects appeared on one of the dunes. They were obscured in the mirages that circled him in all directions but he could tell that one was black and the other white. Perhaps it was the magician with the camel? Nonsense thought he – that was all from a dream. He decided to approach them. When he got closer to these figures, they took form – forms he happily recognized as that of horses. These horses were very large and one pure black in color, the other white -- Their manes and coats shiny. These horses were obviously well cared-for. John looked around in all directions but the mirages revealed no other living things for as far as he could see. They must have escaped from a caravan and lost their way. John knew horses could always find their way home even if they seemed desperately lost. John gave them each a pat on the snout and a kiss. These were very tame horses and obviously raised in a loving environment. It was a shame that John could not help them find their owners. He always did this in Ireland. He did not know the terrain here though so he would only do the horses more harm than good. John returned back to his tent to gather his things. Unless another magic camel appeared, he would have to haul all of it back to Shraugh himself.

When John was done packing, he looked around and saw that the horses had followed him to his camp. He had a the perfect idea then. Since he could not ascertain the direction he needed to follow (The sun was directly overhead now so his shadow gave him no clues), he would pack these horses and let them lead him to their owners. Perhaps those people could give him a map or directions to Cairo. Brilliant! He loaded up the horses quietly. They seemed calm and familiar with this notion and acquiesced. He mounted the black horse but he would switch every hour for however long this took.

Once mounted, both horses began to walk immediately in the same direction. Though there were no reigns, saddle, or stirrups, John felt strangely comfortable. In Shraugh, a boy learns to guide a horse using the mane only and these manes were long and beautiful. This was his expertise and not a worry did he have. John sure had been getting lucky!

The horses began now a slow gallop and gradually increased in speed. They did this seamlessly and John did not even notice them hit full stride. They seemed to know where they were going and judging from the fine state of them, they could not be far from their destination. With any more luck, John would be on trains and ships again headed back to Shraugh within the week. This long adventure might turn out to be the best, if not the most unbelievable, he had ever had. Sure John would be telling this one around many a fire and pub!

After a time of travel over the sands, the horses tackling the dunes with ease, John noticed a long dark streak across the horizon in the direction the horses were headed. The horses galloped harder. They must be close to a large city with rail service. He would spend the night there as he would be a guest and an obvious hero by the town folk. There would certainly be a large party and John was bursting to tell tale of this strange quest. This was a perfect ending to it all save for the look on Carolyn's face when he presented the Ganesh. This was one for the old fables.

A bit further and the dark line on the horizon began growing. Perhaps this was a very large, bustling city and possibly these were the king's horses. Oh, how he would be lauded for returning such fine animals to the king. John let his Irish imagination steal away with him and take him to a daydream of a palace, fine clothes, a large bath, a meal fit for a hero, dancing and drink to exotic music, the finest and most beautiful women of the region feeding him strange fruits and filling his cup and the king and court held rapt with his amazing feats. Such a story he'd never tell on Maeve and he would never betray her. This one was for the pubs only though!

The horses galloped still faster...

John was released from his fantasy in a rather abrupt way. It came in the form of a strong wind and the burn of driven sand across his face. He could barely see the city now as night was beginning to fall. The horses slowed their gait then stopped in front of a small, seemingly abandoned hovel. He dismounted to peruse this place and saw that it was large enough for both he and the horses. He decided that this would be a good place to elude the winds and to spend the night. He would make it to the city in the morning.

After a short meal and the watering of the horses, John leaned back with his pipe around the small fire he had built. He listened to the music the driving winds were composing outside. It was far more melodic than that caterwallerin' old man Quint expelled back at Ginty's in Shraugh! He drifted off as did the horses. He was almost home.

John was awoken in the night by the horses braying. He had no idea of the time and the storm was long passed. The horses had gone outside and he could see them illuminated in the moonlight. THE MOON! From his dreams he remembered this foretelling. He ran out and looked straight up to find it and as sure as he was told, there were two stars configured around it. Though there were thousands of stars visible, these stood out from the rest – the glare of the moon seemed to have no effect on their blaze. He had seen this before but where? AH, the amulet! He peered at it and it had one small symbol embossed there near the its top – two stars with the moon just beneath. It seemed an arrow of sorts that pointed to other bits of obscure writings and symbols emblazoned on the amulet including what seemed a flame. John had never really looked at the amulet before. This was not the last vision he was granted from his dreams but so far everything revealed to him had come to pass. He was rested, the horses were rested – they were ready to go. Tonight they would follow this "arrow" in the sky. Onward they pressed...

This night was staggeringly beautiful—better than any he could remember. Though he tried to guide the horses at first, they shrugged him off and continued in the direction they had maintained throughout. John noticed that this was in direct alignment with that of the moon and stars above. This was interesting but now John could relax and take in the purple panorama around him. What a fool he not to have a pencil and sheet handy to record this. It did not matter. He would not forget and he knew that any embellishment of it would be quite the challenge. John lived for moments like this.

John and the horses continued this routine of resting by day and travelling at night with her moon and stars. He had long forgotten any notions of king's feasts and decadent celebrations in his name. The city was no longer in sight. Other interesting things did he notice though. Through these nights, many different sorts of large and seemingly dangerous animals did he see. He'd read of them before and heard many a tale around the trader's fires of how they could strip a man to bone at that shake of a lamb's tail. These animals did not seem fearsome or dangerous at all. If anything, they avoided his little band -- merely showing curiosity at their passing. "Boy oh Boy if one of them trader's didn't put one over my feeble wee head." thought John. It's a fool of a man to be tellin' such fibs on an Irishman though John had done the like and even worse. An Irishman is never wrong or bested of course.

The dunes and deserts seemed to yield to vast plains of grasses and tall trees. John and the horses were also made to ford many streams and even rivers at several points. This seemed necessary as the horses, moon, and stars were still in exact alignment. He saw an odd creature there very tall, with legs to rival those of any of the gorgeous lasses at the BurleeQs of Paris. Now he had heard tale of such beasts back in Shraugh from that old codger Araigh down at Ginty's. He was told that they were taller than any mountain of Kerry with fangs they gnashed to shame thunder and horns meant to tear flesh even from the Kraken. Their speckled and spotted hides more red than the fires of perdition. They'd hooves crafted after those of the dark lord and "The Devil's Cavalry" Araigh claimed them. No fear of running should one spy you. Pray to St. Daniel and await your immediate fate. "Juraf" Araigh called them – the silly sot. They were an impressive sight but also very timid. John did not attempt to approach them as the horses would not have it or any redirection. He would sure be after tellin' down that Araigh soon!

Came the eve when the horses stopped and would go no further. The foliage was very dense now with many odd sounds emanating from it. All of John's prodding but the horses would not budge. He also saw that moon and stars had disappeared now. Was this the grand "Green Fire" the dreams and magician had spoken of? He could not contain his disappointment. He, an Irishman, was sure-fooled by playful Arabs and a possible witch in their cahoots. A fool he felt. He took a moment but then decided to lead the horses away from this place. He could still get them safe by just following one the rivers they had crossed. He was bound to find a village or town.

Again, the horses would not move in any direction with whatever prodding he could muster. His consternation now doubled. He would wait until morning and let the horses rest. He could figure this out then. He certainly would leave this part of his odyssey unchronicled. They would crucify him with laughter down at Ginty's should this be told. John would not sleep this night though.

As he lay down for a pipe and a fire, he heard a distinct chattering sound around him and a commotion in the foliage. He approached this curiously. He could not sleep now anyway. As he got closer, a small furry creature appeared before him. John had never seen such an animal either in book or zoo. It was indeed the source of the chattering and gave an exclamation with a long "whooooop!". The creature seemed to be inviting a treat from John. He quickly went and got his largest bag where he knew he might have something fit to tithe to this odd fellow. It accepted his gift and began to prance in the strangest ways. It could fly through the dense foliage like a fish in the water and with great leaping bounds. John watched in amazement. Perhaps he could rescue himself down at Ginty's with this part of the story.

After much prancing and showing off, the creature approached John. He offered it another treat as it was well worth the show it put on. The creature refused. Instead, to John's terrible surprise, it reached out and took John's hand. The creature gently pulled him closer to the foliage. John tried to stop but the creature was quite insistent. The creature seemed extremely interested in John's amulet. It must like shiny things.

John followed the creature still further into the thicket. It was there that he discerned an obscure path. Curiosity began to take hold of him and he moved still forward within. The creature released him now and continued its whimsical leaps and prancing in the foliage around the path John was treading. The creature might disappear for short moments but it always was there waiting with a sentinel chirp to prod John to catch up. John continued to follow.

After much time had passed, John had no way of knowing whether it was night or day due to the thick canopy that the foliage had become, he and his unusual new friend came to a clearing on a hillside. It was clearly day time now. From some thickets on the top of the hill came another unheard-of creature John had never seen before. It was larger than John and very wide. It also very much resembled John's new companion (The creature leading John was nowhere to be found at the moment). This larger creature approached John slowly and seemed angry at John's arrival. It charged at John screaming and tearing apart the various thickets in transit. John held his ground and did not falter or break gaze. This had more to do with his shock and amazement than anything involving courage. He would change that bit when he was at Ginty's again but he had more pressing business at hand.

This beast slowed and stopped. John could reach out to touch it and he could also smell its breath. It stared at John intensely and seemed to respect the fact that John did not flee its approach. Its gaze slowly moved down to the amulet around John's neck where it was held for several moments. The beast let out a cry but this time not to summon fear. It seemed an acceptance of sorts. After this, the beast slowly retreated back up the hill past the artwork it had created upon the thickets. John noticed that though the beast was black in color, its back was more silver than any fine bracelet the Queen might have in her coffers at Buckingham. Such strange animals in this place!

John took a moment to ponder this but was finally able to see the opening in the foliage at the other side of the thicket so he decided to go that way. There must be someone here blazing these trails and they could help. When he reached the entrance back into the canopy, he heard the familiar chirp and whooshing of the branches his friend was so fond of presenting as salutation. They took to the trail again and the canopy was becoming darker.

Three days and nights they travelled still further still down this path. John encountered many other amusing animals along the way including a pig that could walk on its knees. He could no longer blame the potions for these sights. Each appearance John eagerly awaited – His curiosity was in full control now.

On one night, his friend stopped on the path with a chirp. It would go no further. John tried a treat but the animal would not budge. It reminded him of the horses. THE HORSES! John had forgotten them. What a piteous state he was in now. John saw the path clearly ahead of him and he would fix it all. He let his friend rest there and carried on. They had travelled so far that the end must be close. His friend could catch up later. As John walked farther down the path, he would stop and glance over his shoulder. His friend was staring at him from the same spot it had stopped. A bit more down the way and the glance – His friend had disappeared again.

John walked for much time this way. He missed his precocious little friend. It was unusual for it to be absent from his company for so long. He entertained the notion of going back to look for it considering the perils they had encountered – that beast in the clearing would make a fine morsel of his friend. As he meandered around a decision, John noticed a flash just a distance up the path – then a second. Perhaps his friend was scared of such things. It surely would explain why it lived in this darkness and why it was not in attendance at the beast encounter on the hill. John would go investigate this flash. Perhaps it was the way out of here.

John precariously ventured down the path – always was looking again for the flash. He then discovered something quite unusual in the air. It was music. He must be near now to another human face. They could help him with the horses and for an egress from this oppressive and endless canopy. John walked over a small rise of the road and what he saw took him aback. It was making sense now.

A fire blazed near a cave just below him. It burned a color more green than all of the land of his upbringing. The music was louder now and he could hear voices, human voices, laughing and rejoicing. "At least they are friendly people" thought John. He approached this place and gazed intently at the fire -- mesmerized. John noticed that this fire was warm but not hot. He put his hand into it and it felt like a tepid bath after a long day's ride. He felt it all over and head to toe. What John did not notice was the medicine man now standing across the fire from him. This man had a great smile upon his face and the party in the cave became even louder. The amulet around his neck was now lighter than goose down...

John and the medicine man shared a long gaze – the shaman's smile never fading. Though this was an awkward moment for John being so far from home, he felt very welcomed and comforted. John decided to raise a hand and lend a greeting. The shaman reciprocated in kind. John began to think of words to say to keep this meeting amicable but the shaman interrupted this with some simple words – "I know why you have come.".

As with the magician, this shaman spoke perfect English and seemed to know all about John's quest. What John did not know is that the shaman wasn't speaking English at all – he understood it perfectly though.

The shaman lowered his hand and entered the cave. The party was extremely lively at this point. "Is he inviting me in?" thought he. John decided he best stay right there by the strange warm fire and await the shaman's return. Only a few moments later or so to John, still enthralled with the fire, and the shaman returned with a large and slightly weath-ered chest. He placed this at John's feet and bade him open it. Taking his gaze away from the fire, John also smiled. What he was going to see next would change the Catlin world and Shraugh for eternity...

John examined the chest. It was tattered from how long ago but otherwise in very fine condition. He opened it and the green fire let off a flare to illuminate the contents. Inside there seemed to be many small figurines – all about the size of a 4 week old kitten. John looked more closely and these were figurines of animals – all of the animals he had encountered on his long journey. There was the white camel, the horses, the "Juraf" (Araigh, ya sot), a "water horse" (Hippopotamus) of which he had seen many in the various rivers, his friend from the canopy, the silver-backed beast from the hill, and the pig that walks on its knees. There was one figure he had not seen on this journey but recognized it immediately as a lion. He picked this one up to examine it further under the warm flare of the green fire.

He saw the extreme quality of this piece. It was of a material he had never encountered before and it was as weightless as the amulet now. This certainly was not a toy, a figurine, or statuette – it was something far different. It was perfect in every detail and a masterpiece of artisan hands. John went on and inspected each of the objects in this worn chest in kind. He found in amazement that they were all in such a state. More confounding to John was that each was an exact copy of the creatures he had met along his trek. They were almost too beautiful to behold and obviously ancient and priceless. What was this gift? At least he now would have proof for the fellas down at Ginty's sure he would. His head was dizzying now.

He placed the last piece gently into its chest and took a moment to consider the lot of them. Reeling, he looked up to see the shaman still smiling at him. John summoned the strength to speak with this man but he was interrupted in mid-thought yet again. The shaman said just one word –"YALI". To John's astonishment, the shaman simply walked away into the darkness with that was now the cave. He could hear no more laughter or music from the cave as it was black and silent. The fire also ebbed and extinguished. It was pitch black all around and no sound—not even from the canopy. John had heard many fantastic old tales of wizards and witchcraft but even for an Irishman, this was too much. John swooned and collapsed there in the darkness.

After however long, John awoke again in his tent. His packs and collections neatly ordered around him as usual but now with the addition of the chest. He was far from being surprised anymore so he just accepted this in a pensive way. It was then he heard the familiar chirp of his friend so he stepped outside to find him. The tent was pitched at the entrance to the canopy where this leg of the journey had landed him. Just inside, he spied his little friend staring at him. John quickly fetched a treat and gave it to the accepting creature. His friend let out one more "Whoop!" then bounded seamlessly deep back into the canopy. John gave a wave and realized that he would never see his friend again.

John turned back to his tent and in front of him were the horses gently whinnying. This was great news to know that they were safe and looking as healthy and beautiful as ever! Each horse also received a treat and waited for John to pack them up. This John did. They would take him to their next destination and John could finally get home now.

They travelled many days and nights past all of the rivers, thickets, plains and dunes just as their approach to this place. The horses did not need rest now so the time went by quickly. John was able to discern the mirages again and recognized this place. Again in the mirage he saw he saw a white figure in the distance – to this was the course they were taking.

On a familiar dune, the horses abruptly stopped again. John knew this meant that they would go no further. He made no attempt to cajole them this time. This was another goodbye and though the tears welled, he realized that this is how it needed to be. He unpacked them and gave each a pat and kiss on the nose with a whispered prayer. He proceeded toward the figure in the mirage and did not look back.

As John had garnered based these past events, he was not surprised when the figure in the mirage slowly took the form of the white camel. He almost expected it. The camel was patient as John packed it up and soon after a mounting, they were headed to another of the predetermined destinations. John had learned to stop fighting and worrying about such things. He knew his journey was nearing the end.

The camel kept its unusual restless gait forward. Many days this travel took but time was lost on John – too many things remembered. Came the day when yet another dark streak appeared on the horizon through the mirages. He knew what his meant. A bit further and expectedly, the camel stopped with another bray. John resigned himself to this and dismounted the magical creature. He quickly unpacked and decided to leave the tent behind him. He would not need that anymore -- not after this trek. Again he gave a pat, kiss, and whispered prayer as his third goodbye and thank you. The camel stared for a moment but then headed off back into the desert. John waited for it to cross over a dune and out of sight. They would never meet again. "Farewell, old friend" was all he could think as he gathered his things to venture towards the dark streak on the horizon.

The rest was a blur for John. He remembered the large city of Cairo and the mailing of all the posts for which he was tardy. He knew his family would be worrying sure by now. John could recall no further the events of that day there and he had entered into a dream.

He was awoken by a loud voice stating "Next stop! Ennis!". He was back in Ireland now on a train and just in time to catch the bus to Shraugh. Never had this island been more beautiful for him. Though exhausted, he was excited to see Mary, Charlotte, and especially, Carolyn. He would get home, enjoy fine home-cooked stew, a pipe by the hearth and fire, and then the stories and gifts. He would then sleep for three days. Araigh and the fellas at Ginty's could wait.

Carolyn's
Circus

Over a last hill in the village that housed that den of corruption of words and lies, Ginty's, he could see just far enough to the place where the bus was to deliver him. His excitement was fountaining now. A few bumps more and there was the glory of his dreams in the setting sun seated quite properly at the stop. He knew that after the tales he had spun in his posts that Carolyn would be punctual. She looked his own heart!

John gathered his things and exited the bus. Carolyn and he exchanged a mutual gaze before he approached her with a smile. "Hello, father" said she. He kissed her and offered a bag to carry – the bag with the Ganesh. Carolyn took the bag and inquired of its contents quizzically frowning. John made a wry smile and said "Something special for you, my dove, as you asked." Carolyn said "Thank you, father." John's smile widened at this for he knew that would be last time she would ever use that term to address him. John also had a priceless chest of goods in his bag that would ensure that Carolyn never would want for anything ever again. It would go for millions in London or in Geneva. Mary and Charlotte were on the stoop of the porch all with smiles and he could smell the welcoming vapors of the stew they had summoned for the evening. He could almost feel the warmth of that green fire again. This was going to be a grand night!

After the serving of the meal and a family prayer, they dined on the best stew and bread John had tasted in many years. It was rare for John to take a third portion. Though John wanted to move directly to the hearth to begin the giving of the stories and the gifts, Maeve's sisters insisted on pie and tea. John could barely contain himself but he politely consumed these things too. After, they all moved to the fire as John prepared his presentation – part of which required making his tea "special". He would spin gems tonight grander than any web a spider might present in the morning!

John started slowly by lighting his pipe and having a sip of tea. He could tell these women were excited as well now – all jittery and trembling as at Christmas eve. He reached for a bag and pulled out an odd red bauble. He told tale of the great healing powers it contained especially on the nights of the half-moon. This had been in a Raja's coffers for 1000 years and passed generation to generation. The sisters marveled at its craftsmanship and with many a breath taken over his tale. Before the envious green Charlotte, John gave this gift to Mary. She smiled and kissed John – she also shot a wicked smirk to her sister.

John reached in his bag again and pulled out what appeared to be a small statuette. It seemed to have the body of a man and the head of a bird – perhaps an eagle or a hawk. John explained its ancient secrets to the girls with tales told of kings and their offerings to this god. It was the embodiment of all pharaohs from a lost and great time in Egypt. King Tutenkhamen might've held this piece and prayed to it many times himself! John pleasantly handed this to Charlotte who furtively accepted it with a look of astonishment and awe.

The sisters loved their gifts and held them as infants. Each of them besting the other about the merits of their new magic totems. John's plan was unfolding perfectly. While they fawned and quibbled, John prepared for the harpoon to his daughter's heart. He refilled his tea and re-stoked his pipe. He let the moment settle and came the time for the sisters to return home. They kissed both Carolyn and John many times and followed with a thousand words of thanks. They bundled themselves up and went into the night. John could hear still debating for miles he swore. Carolyn remained perched her mother's reading chair with the focused look to John on her face. Perfect. It was time for him to deliver his promise to her.

John went to the dining table and lit a single bright candle. He bade Carolyn to come sit with him and Carolyn did this promptly. Her curiosity must be just as his was in that far-away desert when he had fought for this rarity so cleverly against the top traders in the world. He reached once more into his bag and placed an object in front of her. She calmly stared at it as John began his epic story of this prize. John was quite emphatic and emotional describing this piece. Its name, its unusual location at the site thousands of leagues from the place of its creation, its immeasurable age, its beauty, and the incredible powers of strength it gave to those in times of darkness. John would have made a fine member of an auction house that eve. John rambled for a century in the ears of Carolyn who continued to intently stare at this marvel. When John had reached the end of his pitch, the candle nearly exhausted, Carolyn slowly reached out and touched it. She turned her gaze back to John, his eyes all welled with tears, and said "Thank you. father.". She said her goodnight and gave a kiss then up the stairs to her room. The Ganesh remained on the table to the candle's last gleam. John sat in the darkness to finish his tea and perhaps another. "Uh oh" he lamented to himself and went to his bed as well.

Though exhausted, John had trouble sleeping. He felt a failure but there must be a reason she had that reaction. Perhaps Carolyn just needed time to absorb the vast amount of knowledge he had imparted to her. The sheer fine beauty of the Ganesh was overwhelming sure. He remembered how he felt when he first saw and touched it. He was a seasoned explorer and had see many such awe-inspiring treasures in his life but this one had the deepest effect on him. Carolyn was still just a little girl and the light he gave her was far too bright. She needed time to digest it. Yeah, that was it. He had tried to move too fast. Carolyn was a studious young girl so she would no doubt research this object for every scrap – then she would understand its incredible magnitude and take it everywhere with her to brag and tell tales of it. When he sold that chest and moved his girl into a great vast mansion with horses and housekeepers and butlers, she would smile for him. Carolyn would never want again.

At this conclusion, John was finally able to rationalize his way to sleep.

John slept till very late the next morning. Part of it was the exhaustions of the travels and part of it was the tea. He slowly got up and dressed before moving to the kitchen for a breakfast. He noticed Carolyn had finished hers earlier and her plate and cutlery were clean and neatly placed on a counter. She had made it to her school punctually as ever. The

Ganesh and the candle were just as they were left from the night before. "Time", he thought, "Time".

John figured this was a good time to make a few calls to his ilk of fine art appraisers and this he did. He described the contents of the chest he was gifted in the canopy and it worked them into lathering. They also spoke of London, Geneva, and a few other top-shelf houses around the world. He would need to show them the merchandise first and this was something he would do today – First, there would be a visit to Ginty's for the dressing-down of that blow-hard, Araigh. He finished his egg and toast then went to go wash up; He had to look his best today!

As he prepared for his visit to the village proper, came a stark conundrum for John. He looked and looked but he could not find his food bag containing the chest. His other satchels of baubles he had still arrayed by the hearth from before but the food bag was missing. Did he leave it on a train or ship? John could barely remember seeing it since before Cairo and the voyage to here was lost in a dark protracted sleep. He made a quick call to the station but no report of a missing bag of any kind on any of the trains to Ennis. They had found a scarf though. Did he leave it on the ship or worse the streets of Cairo? If so, it was in the Queen's coffers now and lost forever.

John took this hope for solace to Ginty's but not even the soon-to-be-lambasted Araigh was there. He sat in quiet corner with a pint and tried to retrace his steps. It was the second most important treasure he had procured. He let the day pass this way. It was nearly time for Carolyn to return from her school so he must get home and cook a meal. He left just as Araigh arrived with more snide boasts or invitations and John no chance to defeat them. Ah, could his day get any worse?

He travelled back to the cottage to wait for Carolyn at the bus stop and the bus was right on-time. Carolyn was not present though. Perhaps the pints had muddled his mind as to the schedule so he returned to cottage to begin preparing a meal. Tonight would be leftovers from last night's delicious stew and it would be easy. As the stew simmered and the bread warmed, he searched his home for a second time – The Ganesh and candle still in their usual places seeming to mock him. He realized that he had one more gift he had not thought of, it was the amulet around his neck. It was still there and light as a feather.

After an hour or so, he heard the door open and the pleasant clomping of Carolyn's school shoes. He welcomed her again with a smile and kiss as they sat down to eat. He asked her about her day as one does and Carolyn spoke again. She was sitting near the Ganesh so perhaps it was starting to affect her. This was one good sign for such a dreary and confusing day.

At the conclusion of the meal, John addressed Carolyn one more time. He said "My dove, I've brought to you this amulet from the darkest Congo canopies. It contains a strange magic as he went on to tell tale of his adventures there. He placed the necklace around the curious Carolyn's neck with another kiss on her forehead. Carolyn regarded it and smiled properly for the first time in a coon's age. She hugged him and peeped to him "Thank you, daddy.".

"DADDY?!? DADDY ?!? John's head was reeling with joy now. He trembled a smile and hugged her as gently as was possible for a man in his state. To take things further, Carolyn made one more request of her father that would make him hear the wing-beats of angels. Carolyn slowly reached over and touched the Ganesh before looking up and asking "daddy, can he come up and play with me tonight? I will bring him back in the morning". John ran out words of how to say "yes" and that is difficult for an Irishman. He said "You don't need to bring him back. Keep him by your side, always." He was welling up again and it front of his daughter was no place to weep. Carolyn took the Ganesh and scampered up the stairs to her room. John went to the hearth and lit his pipe before retiring to his room.

In his bed, now content, John looked upon the odd happenings of the day. It had started so terribly after the misplacing of the chest and was made worse by the ramblings of that codger, Araigh. A flash of heaven was he envisioning now. As John slowly made the humble submission from waking to sleep, he heard playful scrabbling and Carolyn's laughter from the room above. If there are rats up there then they are welcome to stay. That night, John fell into dreams with a smile on his face. This was the first time since before Mauve was summoned away.

John woke in the morning refreshed. He had time to make Carolyn's breakfast and get her off to school. The lone candle was a memory from the night before and a fine one. He left it where it was. He looked as his watch and oddly, Carolyn had not emerged from her chambers yet. It was a big night for her too so she must've slept in a bit longer. John sure knew that feeling.He went up the hallway stairs to her room to check on her. What he saw would give him both a mix of cheer and shock greater than any Arab potion.

John knocked on Carolyn's door but not a peep did he hear. He opened it and there was Carolyn fast asleep with a stunning grin. To her left on the nightstand, he saw the Ganesh. The statue was pointed directly at her where she had left him for the night.What really caught John's attention, and he had to rub his eyes, was the vision of the open chest he had brought home. The contents of the chest were spread all over the room. He also saw that Carolyn had forgot to hang her school clothes from the day before. He slowly put each piece of finery back into the chest carefully before closing it. He then gently nudged Carolyn to rouse her. She smiled and said "Good morning, daddy". He smiled and left her to get dressed. He went back downstairs to serve breakfast and it would be a small one as Carolyn was becoming dangerously close for a school tardiness. He had more to ponder now.

"So Carolyn came and took the chest in the night. She was as enamored with the contents the same as I was at first sight of them. She played with them all through the night and was smiling and calling me 'daddy' again." went in John's mind. He would explain the situation to her later. These were priceless pieces meant to deliver them from poverty and shame he must cast on the little dickens to be after pilfering them in the shadows. John was not very good at punishing Carolyn so for today, he would not speak of it. What he saw in her bedroom was of such absolute beauty that it would be hard for him to kill it for his goals of gaining vast riches. This admonishment must be crafted however. He had to stay strong and be the father. It sure did not sit right with him but he must fight this weakness. He was resolute.

Carolyn began returning notes again from the school. These were not so praising as before and she starting being late again and disheveled. She always had a smile and laughed though. She was transforming into the Carolyn of old before his very eyes. John was still not sure how to punish her nor could find a good reason to perform it. He would give it a few more days to mull it over. He would have to confront her soon though. The appraisers were waiting.

Many days and weeks began to pass this way. Each day and night Carolyn and he would eat breakfast and later dinner. They would have happy cheery talks and she loved his recounting of the trials he had faced on this last journey. He loved to tell the Congo story to Carolyn who was so bubbling with the questions and transfixed with the answers he revealed. This stroked John's ego but in the back of his mind, doom was looming. After Carolyn had her fill of stories, she would proceed to her room and he to the hearth. Each night he could hear the scrabbling and the laughter and each morning he had to rise and wake her – the fine pieces always strewn about the room and he always collected and replaced them into the chest. This was still fine with John though he knew he had bills to pay and the collection upstairs must depart soon. He was also very curious about the laughter and play he heard throughout the night. In the morning, he would address Carolyn.

The morning did come where John made breakfast, went upstairs, cleaned up the priceless treasures tossed about, to awaken Carolyn. She washed, dressed, and came down the stairwell, her eyes and smile still gleaming from the night before, and took her seat. On this morning, John knew he was certain to erase that smile from her face. This was probably the hardest thing John would have to do in his whole life. He allowed Carolyn to begin her meal -- she was still smiling.

John finally took the leap and uttered "My angel, I notice that you have purloined something from me.". Carolyn did not look up and her smile widened. "Carolyn, they are very beautiful, the pieces in that chest, yes?" said brave John. Carolyn looked up and said "Yes, daddy" through her oat-meal-smeared smile. "My dove, it is not okay for you to sneak around in the dark and steal from others. You know this, yes?" -- John was out on the limb now. She looked up again and said "Yes, daddy." through another smile. John had hit a wall so it was time to get to his point. "Darlingest, you are free to play with them each and every night under one con-dition – that you safely put them up before you go to sleep." Another smile and a "Yes, daddy." Now John was ready to strike. "Carolyn, that chest and pieces it contains must leave soon. They will bring to us great profit and to you a horse of your own and a grand room with butlers and servants and all you want!". Carolyn's smile faded briefly but with a "Yes, daddy." John's cat was out of the bag and he had gone too far with her too soon. He needed to rescue this and quickly. John mustered from a soft part of his heart where a backpedal he could always find, "...but if you take good care of them, I see no problem with you keeping them safe for me. If you abuse them, I will be made to take them away. Do you understand?". Carolyn's smile returned immediately. She replied "Yes, daddy." She jumped up and hugged him before skipping off to school. She had left her food half-eaten and dishes on the table. This was certainly his Carolyn again.

These days went on and the patterns for John and Carolyn repeated. Again, "Time", is what John thought just as with the Ganesh. Carolyn would adhere to his directive soon. At night, John always heard the playing and bumping from upstairs. Now it was more the curiosity that was getting to John. His daughter was happy again and no longer deeply pensive. The more adverse notes Carolyn got from the school? To John's life scrapbook they went next his more illustrious recounts of deeds past. He was also happy to be scrubbing the mud off her clothing again. Carolyn had resumed a tea party of her own now. Children from the village were attending these and also invited were the fantastic inhabitants of that chest -- Ganesh the centerpiece. This was wonderful but John knew he had a dragon to kill soon. The bills were mounting and the appraisers nagging him daily. He would preserve Carolyn's world as long as he could but the day was coming where he would have to pilfer that chest from her room. It would hurt but in the end all of their problems would be solved. This he consoled himself with for a few more nights. He would be gentler than any thief in the night. A contradiction to him he supposed considering the evils of such behavior he pronounced on Carolyn but he knew this was different. He would bring his family the finest with the least tears he could produce. This was right and how it needed to be done.

The call came through one day from the appraisers with the message that several of their most highly touted would be in Dublin for the weekend. They were willing to have audience with John so it was time to strike the iron this night. John went off to Ginty's and lament. "It is okay, John. You warned her and now the time has come. You have been truthful to her throughout." thought him over yet another pint. This would've been exactly the worst time for that blathering Araigh to appear. Blessedly he did not as John could not guarantee a safe end to Araigh's evening.

The afternoon came and John carefully crafted a delicious meal. Carolyn and her friends were out in the meadow laughing and playing as the tea party waned into evening. At its conclusion, John escorted the children to the bus stop or to the trails on fields back to their homes. Carolyn smiled and waved from the window. The poor thing had no idea what was coming -- nor did John.

Carolyn and her father sat down and ate their dinner together. She seemed exhausted but happy. She would sleep soundly tonight and allow him window for his nefarious business without a hitch. Her ire he would deal when he returned from Dublin. After laughter and stories, Carolyn ran up to bedroom as ever. John went to the hearth for a pipe again and let her machinations unfold. He went to his bed and waited for her nightly celebration to cease. She was asleep before midnight tonight and no pattering or laughter did he hear. It was time for him to proceed with his deed.

John removed his boots for stealth and slowly proceeded down the hallway to the staircase. John was stone-faced now in a way that would put Carolyn's previous episodes to shame. As a mouse up the stairs and down the dark hallway he toed gently. He was at Carolyn's door now so he took another listen there – silence.

He slowly turned the handle and opened the door just a crack. He could see Carolyn fast asleep with her unmovable grin. He also saw the Ganesh still perched on her nightstand still pointed at her. Through the small gap, he could see the chest open a few of the pieces scattered around on the floor. He would have to quietly pack them quietly and abscond without so much as a murmer. He expected this. John proceeded to fully open the door and enter to complete his task.

What John saw next held him in his tracks. One of the pieces, illuminated by moon and stars through Carolyn's window, seemed to be staring at him. It had eyes that glowed like the embers of a freshly extinguished fire. The piece was deadly still and John was mesmerized at how the light could create this amazing effect. John's aspirations of amazing riches and glory beyond all means were about to be crushed forever.

After a long gaze, John noticed the eyes blink. Could this be? It was late and he was tired too. Perhaps it was he that had blinked. There was no mistaking the sight John beheld when the figure and eyes began to move towards Carolyn's bed. In a single bound, it lept up and moved to curl up on Carolyn's chest. The moon and stars illuminated it. It was the lion. It rested there and began to purr – all the while keeping that stare on the dumbfounded John. His thoughts raced out of control. What had he done? What is that? Did he bring some class of evil African spirit to his daughter? Why had the medicine man smiled so? Are we cursed now? "WHAT HAVE I DONE?" John's mind shouted. John slowly backed away from this spectacle. He would fix it all in the morning forever. The appraisers called and certainly not a moment too late. This abomination must go.

As he began to close the door, he saw Carolyn shuffle a bit in her bed. Her arm came out from under the covers and embraced the purring lion still staring intensely at her father. She whispered one thing from her dreams and with a knowing smile...

"I love you, Mother."

The End...